SLEEPING BOY

SLEEPING

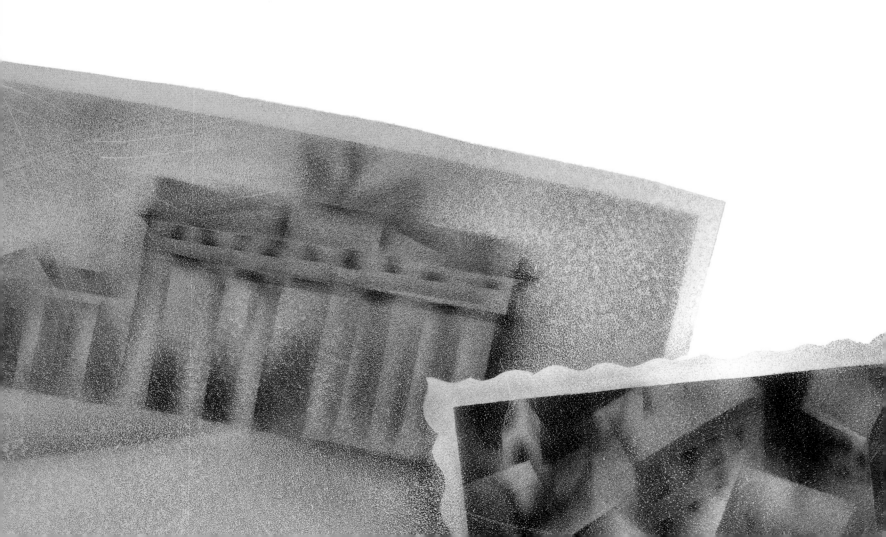

BOY

written by Sonia Craddock
illustrated by Leonid Gore

ATHENEUM BOOKS FOR YOUNG READERS

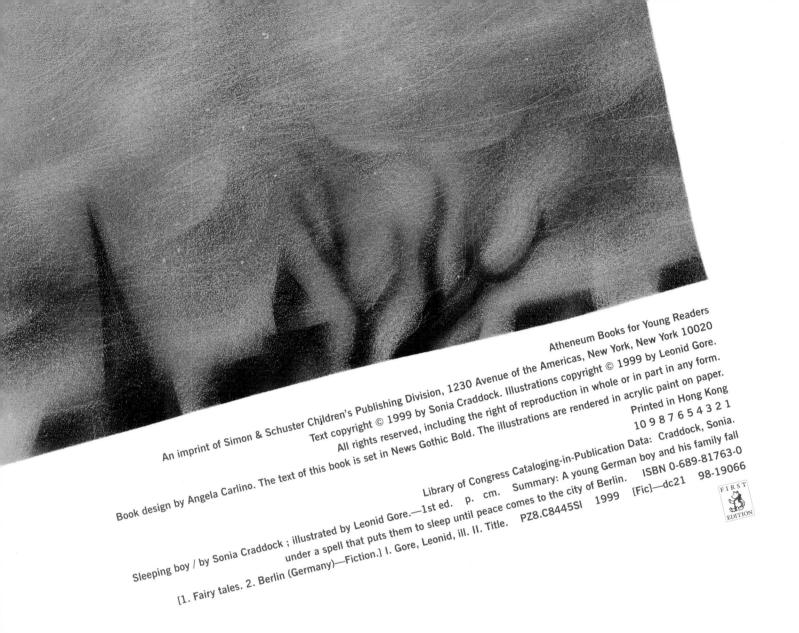

Atheneum Books for Young Readers

An imprint of Simon & Schuster Children's Publishing Division, 1230 Avenue of the Americas, New York, New York 10020

Text copyright © 1999 by Sonia Craddock. Illustrations copyright © 1999 by Leonid Gore.

Printed in Hong Kong

Book design by Angela Carlino. The text of this book is set in News Gothic Bold. The illustrations are rendered in acrylic paint on paper.

10 9 8 7 6 5 4 3 2 1

Library of Congress Cataloging-in-Publication Data: Craddock, Sonia.

Sleeping boy / by Sonia Craddock ; illustrated by Leonid Gore.—1st ed.   p.   cm.   Summary: A young German boy and his family fall under a spell that puts them to sleep until peace comes to the city of Berlin.   ISBN 0-689-81763-0

[1. Fairy tales. 2. Berlin (Germany)—Fiction.] I. Gore, Leonid, ill. II. Title.   PZ8.C8445Sl   1999   [Fic]—dc21   98-19066

FIRST
EDITION

To Kieran James

—S. C.

To Misha

—L. G.

Laugh and smile.
Smile and laugh.
That's Herr and Frau Rosen.
And don't they think they are happy—
Yes indeed!

And don't they think their house is something. Surely the narrowest house in Berlin, all shy and sleepy, and so squashed between grand villas that it can hardly breathe. Well, they love it, so that's all right.

And when their baby boy is born. Well! That is something else! What a fuss! What a commotion! What a party to celebrate! Every friend and acquaintance they have is invited. Well, nearly everyone. They leave out Major Krieg. They don't like him. He makes them feel uneasy. And once upon a time he'd wanted to marry Frau Rosen, and she'd turned him down flat. The Major has never forgiven her. Never. Still, it is a mistake to ignore him.

Oh, but it's cold outside. Hail and sleet all over. The horses are slipping and sliding on the cobbles. The grand housefronts are shuttered tight, and the delivery boys are shivering icicles.

Ah, but inside. It's all pink and warm. See the fine clothes, the food and the drink and the glittering glass. It's just too much. The servants are quite run off their feet.

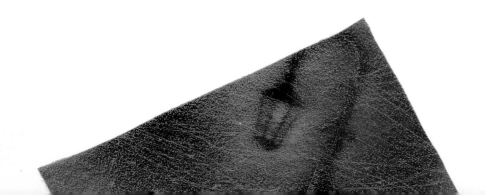

"A toast!" cries Herr Rosen, stout and beaming. "A toast to our sleeping boy, our Knabe Rosen."

"Sleeping boy!" cry the guests. They raise their glasses to the new baby, and the chandeliers tinkle merrily, to and fro.

"Such a good baby," says Frau Rosen, plump and pretty. And so he is.

And then the guests step forward with their blessings. "I wish Knabe Rosen a long life," says the first.

"And always good health," says the second.

"With all that he may ask for," says the third.

"Oh dear me," coos Tante Taube, all gray and softness, dropping her knitting and fluttering up from her seat in the corner. "Let me see. What shall I wish?"

"Oh, Tante Taube." They tease her. "What wish can you give?" And they give her a hug and whirl her around, for Tante Taube is one of those poor relations that everyone likes, but she will knit sweaters that are far too big, and when she helps in the kitchen the jellies never set. And, sorry to say, she always gets the hard bed, the cracked plate, and the chair a long way from the stove. But she doesn't mind.

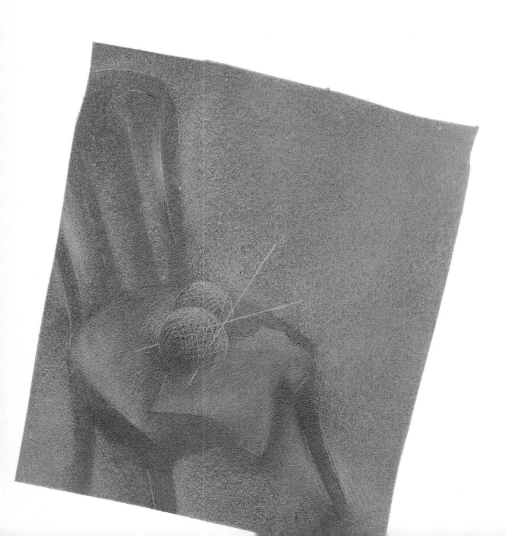

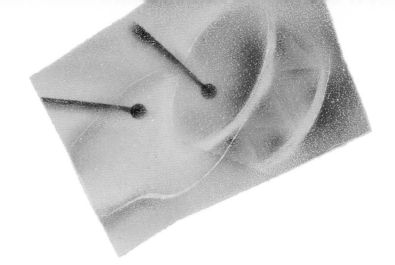

But what's this? Whip lashing, hooves rearing. A black-cloaked rider on a black stallion thunders up to the front door. Servants scurry. "Torches! Quick!" And a voice, sharp and steely, cuts into the night.

"Out of the way, fool!"

"It's Major Krieg!" say the whispers. And the chandeliers flicker wildly, to and fro.

And it is, too. And here he is, black cape swirling, black boots kicking the door, and black eyes blazing.

"Oh, Major Krieg!" Frau Rosen clings to Herr Rosen's hand. "What a surprise!"

"I'm sure it is," says Major Krieg, and he fixes his stare across the room to where Knabe Rosen sleeps softly in the nursemaid's arms. "I've come to give this sleeping boy my blessing."

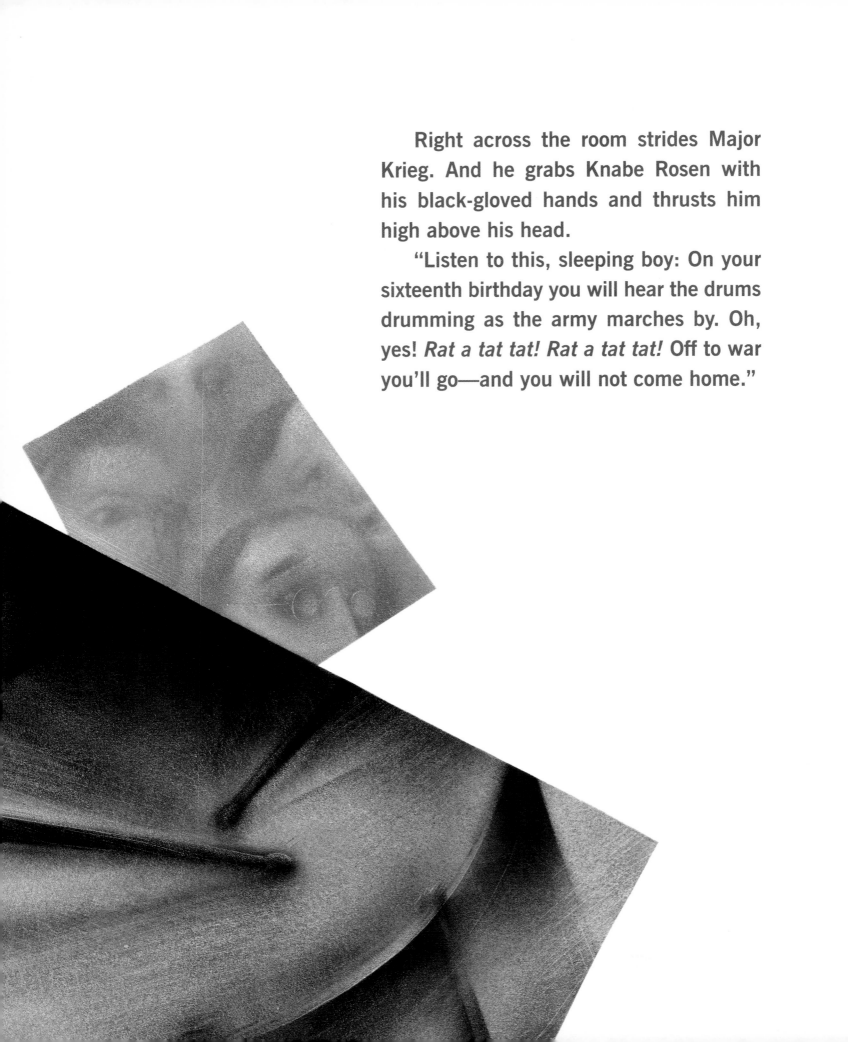

Right across the room strides Major Krieg. And he grabs Knabe Rosen with his black-gloved hands and thrusts him high above his head.

"Listen to this, sleeping boy: On your sixteenth birthday you will hear the drums drumming as the army marches by. Oh, yes! *Rat a tat tat! Rat a tat tat!* Off to war you'll go—and you will not come home."

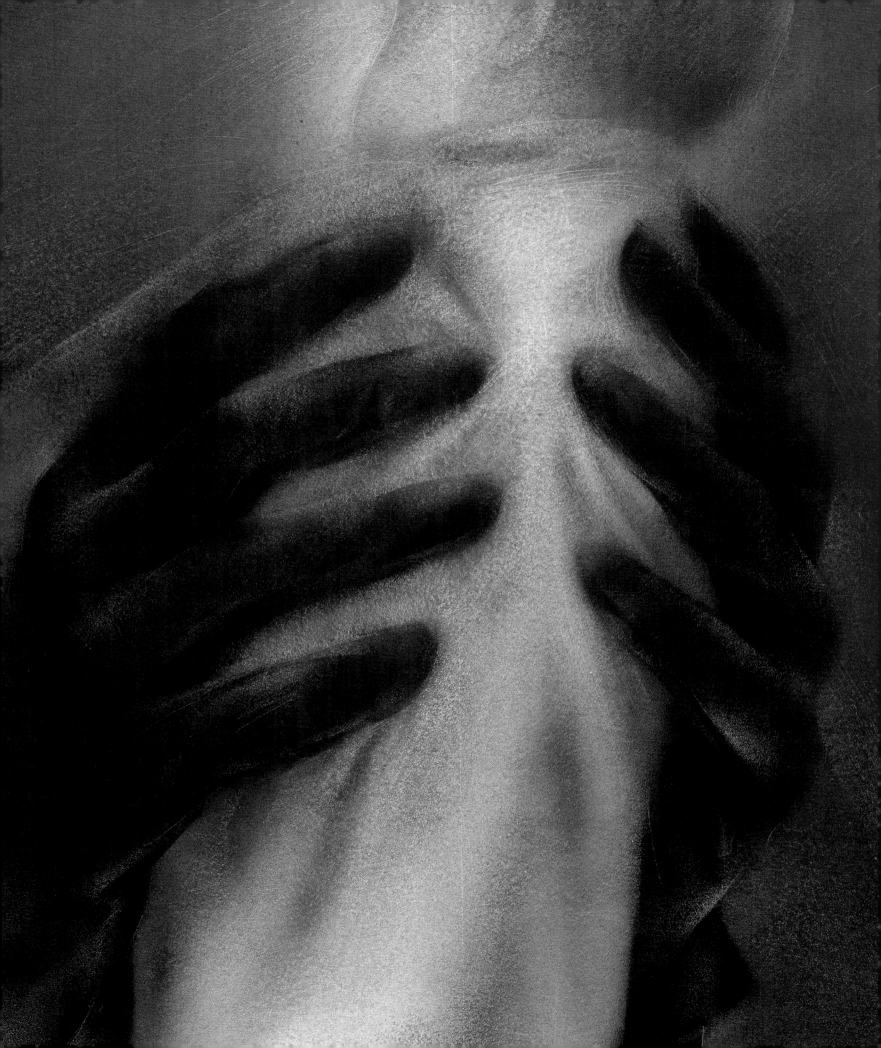

"No!" cries Herr Rosen, white and shaking.

"No!" cries Frau Rosen, faint and swooning.

"No!" cry the guests, wide-eyed and staring.

"No!" cries Tante Taube, soft and weeping.

Too late. Major Krieg tosses the baby at the nurse, turns on his heels, and is gone.

And oh, the room is cold! It's as if winter has come inside. How everyone weeps and wails. "What to do! What to do!" And the chandeliers tinkle sadly, to and fro.

"Well," says Tante Taube. "I haven't given Knabe Rosen my blessing yet. I can't change what Major Krieg has foretold, but . . ." She smiles down at the sleeping boy.

"Oh, Tante Taube!" They chide her. "Go back to your knitting. What can you do?"

But Tante Taube kisses the baby's cheek. "On his sixteenth birthday, when Knabe Rosen hears the drums drumming and the army marching by, he will fall sound asleep. He will sleep through poverty and war, bad times and sadness, until PEACE comes to Berlin."

"Oh, Tante Taube!" Everyone shakes their heads. "What is all this nonsense?"

And everyone turns away.

And, sorry to say, no one heeds Tante Taube at all.

Sad and worried.

Worried and sad.

That's Herr and Frau Rosen.

Herr Rosen summons all the servants. "This is an order. No marching band will be allowed to come down our street."

Frau Rosen, pale and anxious, nods her head. If Knabe Rosen doesn't hear the marching band, he will be safe.

So there it is. When a marching band comes anywhere near the narrow house, a servant is sent outside to order the band to follow another street.

Then Herr Rosen gives another order. "We will have no music in the house. No music at all." Frau Rosen nods her head again. If Knabe Rosen doesn't hear any music at all, he will be safe.

So there it is. It is forbidden to sing, dance, whistle, or play any instrument inside the narrow house. When the kitchen maid forgets and hums a little tune, she is fired immediately. When the butler does a little dance, he is dismissed.

As for Knabe Rosen, well, he is watched over day and night, night and day. Before he can even go into the garden, a servant is sent outside to listen— just in case there is some music in the distance.

Poor Knabe Rosen. He climbs the stairs up to the attic. He stares at the city and watches the world go by. "I see children running in the park. I see children walking with their parents. I see children riding in a carriage. Why can't I do these things, too?" he asks.

"It's not safe," say Herr Rosen and Frau Rosen. But they won't tell him why.

Poor Knabe Rosen. He has three teachers who come to the house. One for lessons, one for art, and one for exercises. But they are middle-aged men, all dour and dutiful.

Poor Knabe Rosen. Once a year the doctor comes to check his health and the dentist comes to check his teeth. But they are both old men, dry and dusty.

The years go by and still no one listens to Tante Taube. "Knabe Rosen will sleep through poverty and war, bad times and sadness, until PEACE comes to Berlin."

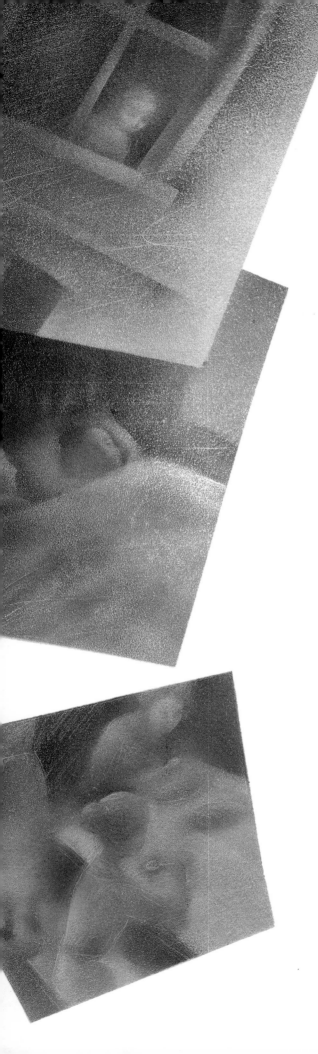

And then comes Knabe Rosen's sixteenth birthday.

A whirling, twirling day with the red and yellow leaves blowing through the autumn air, crisp and clear. Knabe Rosen gazes out of the attic window at the swirling city, and sighs.

Downstairs, everyone else is ill. See Herr Rosen and Frau Rosen in bed, coughing and wheezing. See Tante Taube warming herself by the stove and the servants huddled in the kitchen sipping hot soup—all so muddled they have forgotten this important day.

But what's this? What's that sound? Knabe Rosen has never heard anything like it!

Rat a tat tat! Rat a tat tat! Knabe Rosen pushes the attic window open as far as it will go and sticks his head out into the gusty day.

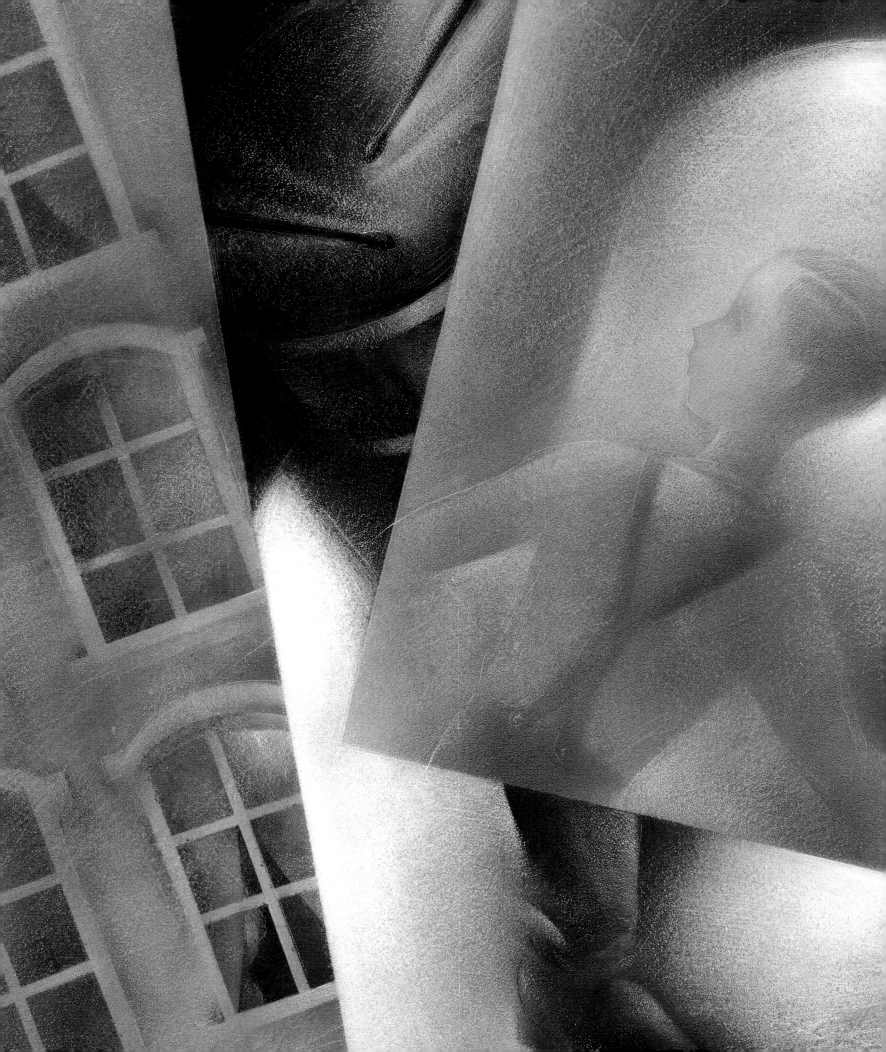

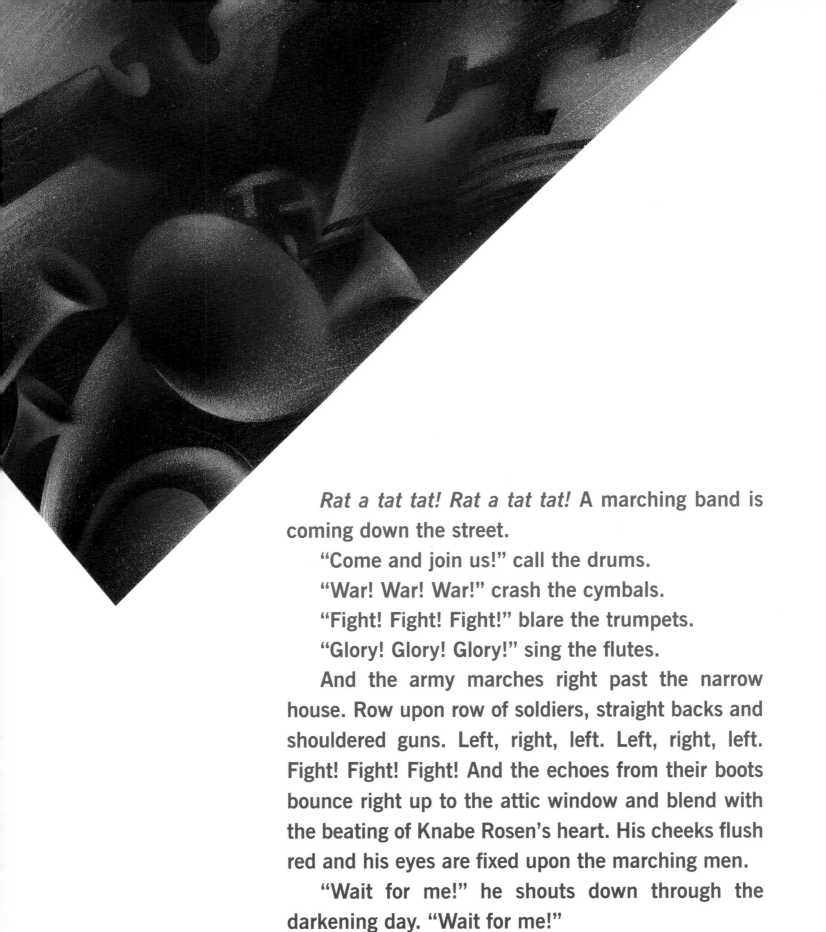

Rat a tat tat! Rat a tat tat! A marching band is coming down the street.

"Come and join us!" call the drums.

"War! War! War!" crash the cymbals.

"Fight! Fight! Fight!" blare the trumpets.

"Glory! Glory! Glory!" sing the flutes.

And the army marches right past the narrow house. Row upon row of soldiers, straight backs and shouldered guns. Left, right, left. Left, right, left. Fight! Fight! Fight! And the echoes from their boots bounce right up to the attic window and blend with the beating of Knabe Rosen's heart. His cheeks flush red and his eyes are fixed upon the marching men.

"Wait for me!" he shouts down through the darkening day. "Wait for me!"

And Knabe Rosen races down the stairs with the drums beating in his head. *Rat a tat tat! Rat a tat tat!* Down the stairs, two at a time, he skids and slides. "Wait for me! Wait for me!" he calls.

But on the tenth stair down he gives a little yawn. On the twelfth stair down he leans against the banister, and just as he gets to the bottom stair of all, he sinks to the ground and his eyes close tight. And the army marches on without him. Left, right, left. Left, right, left. Their boots echo faintly on the cobblestones.

So that's that! Tante Taube's blessing has come to pass. But not quite in the way she wished it. Just as Tante Taube's sweaters never quite fit and her jellies never quite set, so her blessing gets a bit muddled, too. For as Knabe Rosen falls into a deep sleep, so does everyone else in the house as well.

Herr Rosen gives a great sneeze and falls fast asleep, propped against his pillows. Frau Rosen snoozes over her book. Tante Taube snores softly beside the stove. The servants fall asleep in the kitchen. The mice fall asleep in the walls and the kittens fall asleep in the back pantry.

And there they stay.

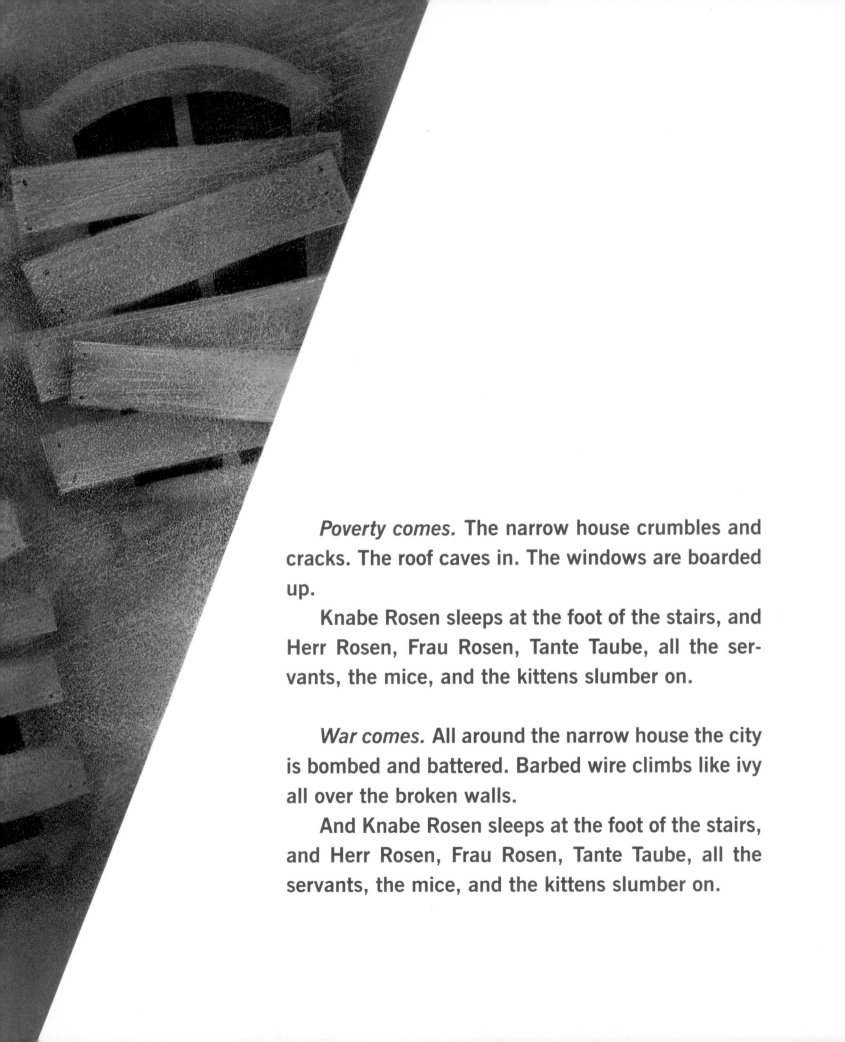

Poverty comes. The narrow house crumbles and cracks. The roof caves in. The windows are boarded up.

Knabe Rosen sleeps at the foot of the stairs, and Herr Rosen, Frau Rosen, Tante Taube, all the servants, the mice, and the kittens slumber on.

War comes. All around the narrow house the city is bombed and battered. Barbed wire climbs like ivy all over the broken walls.

And Knabe Rosen sleeps at the foot of the stairs, and Herr Rosen, Frau Rosen, Tante Taube, all the servants, the mice, and the kittens slumber on.

Bad times come. A huge wall of concrete and steel is built across the city to keep the people apart. Like an angry snake the wall slithers across Berlin, splitting streets and parks, houses and gardens. And the narrow house is surrounded with concrete blocks—and buried right inside the wall. Yes! You wouldn't even know it was there.

And still Knabe Rosen sleeps at the foot of the stairs, and Herr Rosen, Frau Rosen, Tante Taube, all the servants, the mice, and the kittens slumber on.

Sadness comes. All around the buried house is desolation. Guard dogs patrol the wall. Searchlights pierce the sky.

PEACE does not come to Berlin.

Until . . . one day.

What a day!

Thousands of people pour through the streets with music and song. *"PEACETIME IS NOW!"* they cry. And they climb all over the wall, cheering and throwing flowers.

Chip! Chip! Chip! They hammer away at the wall. *Chip! Chip! Chip!* Bands play songs of peace. People hug one another and cry tears of joy.

Chip! Chip! Chip! **PEACETIME IS NOW,** echo the hammers.

Chip! Chip! Chip! **PEACETIME IS NOW,** chime the chisels.

Veins turn to cracks, cracks to gaps—and there's the narrow house, just as ever it was, all shy and sleepy.

And what's this? The front door yawns open and in pours the sun, all gold and dazzling, and in skip some children, all flowers and laughter.

Ah! Ah! Wake up, Knabe Rosen! Wake up, sleeping boy! *PEACETIME* is here.

And inside their best bedroom, Herr and Frau Rosen open their eyes and stretch.

"My," says Herr Rosen, "I feel like I've slept for years."

"How strange. Me, too," says Frau Rosen.

And Tante Taube blinks her eyes and hurries to help with the jellies. The servants shake their heads and start to bustle around. The mice begin to scurry and the kittens mew hungrily for their mother.

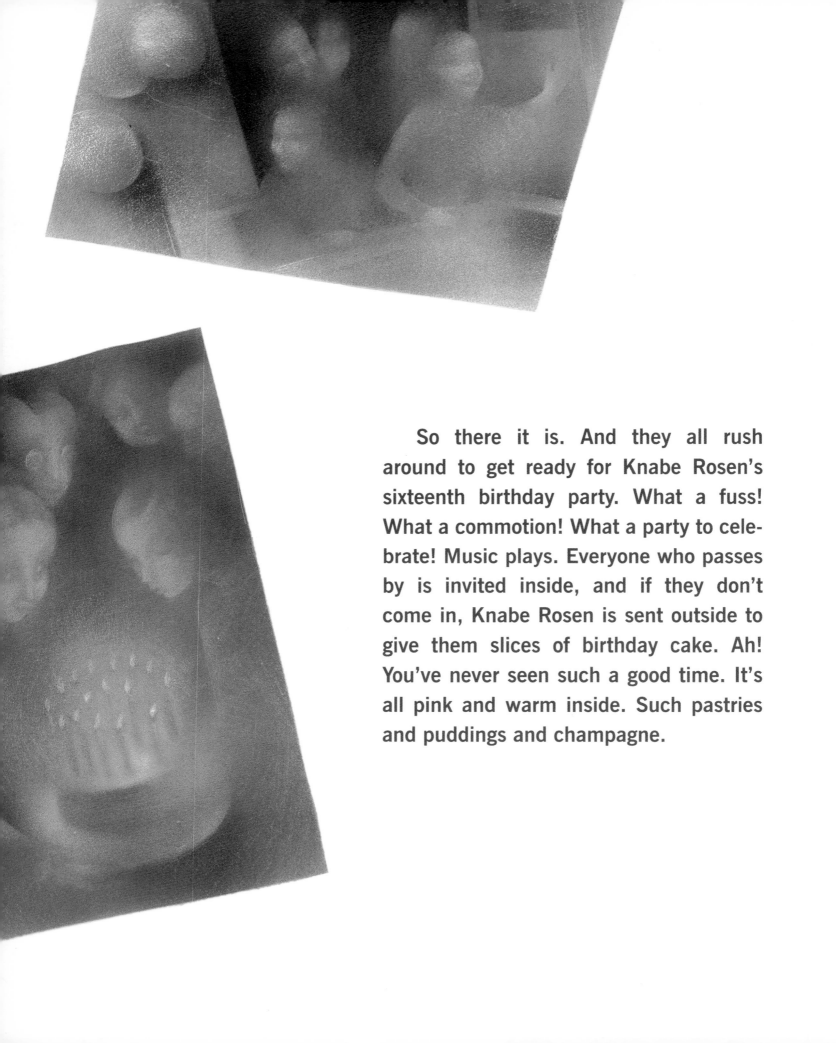

So there it is. And they all rush around to get ready for Knabe Rosen's sixteenth birthday party. What a fuss! What a commotion! What a party to celebrate! Music plays. Everyone who passes by is invited inside, and if they don't come in, Knabe Rosen is sent outside to give them slices of birthday cake. Ah! You've never seen such a good time. It's all pink and warm inside. Such pastries and puddings and champagne.

"Even your jellies have set." They tease Tante Taube. And so they have.

"A toast!" cries Herr Rosen, stout and beaming. "A toast to our Knabe Rosen, and to PEACE."

"Knabe Rosen and PEACE!" cry the guests, and they raise their glasses to each other. And the chandeliers tinkle joyfully, to and fro.

Laugh and smile.
Smile and laugh.
That's Knabe Rosen, sleeping boy.
That's Herr and Frau Rosen, too.
And don't they think they are happy—
Yes indeed!